Lucia Morning in Sweden

By Ewa Rydåker, with illustrations by Carina Ståhlberg
Editor • Anne Gillespie Lewis
Graphic Designer • Inga-Lena Ohlsson

Hej! (hay) = Hi!
Ja (Yah) = Yes
Nej (nay) = No
Sankta Lucia = St. Lucia
Pepparkakor= Ginger snaps
Lussekatter = Lucia buns
Lussekatt = one bun
Tack så mycket (Talk so michah) = Thanks very much
Tomten = Santa
God Jul (good yule) = Merry Christmas

Acknowledgement

It has been several years since the idea for this book came about. After I moved to Minnesota from Uppsala, Sweden, and became active at the American Swedish Institute, I listened to first, second, and even third generations tell wonderful stories about their memories from childhood. I heard American Swedish families ask, "How do you do the Lucia celebration?" and I became aware of how meaningful a book on Swedish traditions would be for children and their parents and grandparents.

Annette Bittner, at the American Swedish Institute, convinced me, when she suggested the need for a Lucia book for children. Without Annette this Lucia book would not have happened. Tack så mycket!

Anne Gillespie Lewis, journalist and author, helped a lot to make this book a reality. She worked with me editing the book and also added her creative ideas to it.

Carina Ståhlberg brought my memories to life with her wonderful illustrations.

The book, to a large extent, reflects how our family celebrated Lucia morning in Uppsala, Sweden, before we moved to Minnesota.

My heartfelt thanks to my supportive husband *Anders*, and our two daughters, *Sofie* and *Louise*, who made the Lucia mornings in Sweden significant, wonderful events that are forever lasting. The yearly Lucia celebration, December 13, was very much loved by my now deceased mother Svea and my father Rune, who still lives in Uppsala.

It would not have been possible to complete this book if an old friend of mine, *Inga-Lena Ohlsson*, the graphic designer of this book, had not found this project appealing. I got reacquainted with my generous friend due to the sister-city relationship between Minneapolis and Uppsala.

Björn Tillman at the printing company Civilen AB was very helpful also.

Many thanks to *Margaretha Hedblom*, Dalarna, Sweden, who always finds answers to my questions and is always positive and cheerful.

Designer *Louise Molin* has kind-heartedly designed the traditional Lucia patterns, and *Kjrsten Holt*, of Control Design in St. Paul, prepared the pattern for the printer.

Thanks also, to my dear friend *Gunhild Anderson*, who passed away before this project was completed. Gunhild´s optimism, her mind, spirit, her thoughts, and advice always felt true and genuine. Gunhild and her husband Hilding meant a lot to me.

Other good friends of mine are *Axel* and *Gudrun Ohman*. Axel, from day one, made me understand that hard work, honesty, and sticking to what you believe in, will help you when you come to this "new land." Thank you.

Some of my friends who listened, encouraged, filled in, and gave me great advice are: *Annika Flood*, *Monica* and *Torbjörn Johansson*, *Ingvar Larsson*, *Gun Lydh*, *Inger Pignolet*, *Robin Rutili*, *Karin Rydåker* and *Folke Rydåker*.

Thanks also to *Bruce Karstadt*, executive director of the American Swedish Institute, who believed in the project.

Lucia Morning in Sweden
Copyright © 2002 Ewa Rydåker
ISBN: 978-1-935666-65-3
Hardcover edition originally published under ISBN 91-631-1730-4 by Ewa Rydåker;
Printed by Civilen AB, Halmstad, Sweden; first printing 2002, second printing 2003.
Printed by Friesens, Alrona, Manatoba, Canada; third printing 2005, fourth printing 2008.
Published 2014 by Nodin Press, 5114 Cedar Lake Road, Minneapolis, MN 55416.
Second Nodin Press printing, 2015
Supported by 👑👑 Swedish Council of America

It is December 12th in Sweden. Snow is piling up outside the Svensson house.
The three Svensson children are excited because this is their favorite time of the year.

"Hej, Mama. It smells like Christmas. What are you baking?"
"Your favorite, Carl, pepparkakor!"

"Tomorrow is a special day. Do you know why?" says Mama.

"I think I know. If you're making pepparkakor, it's almost Christmas, and tomorrow's December 13th. That's Lucia Day!"

"That's right. In Sweden Lucia Day means Christmas is getting close.

5

Sofie and Louise will be coming in soon.

Can you help me get ready to make the Lussekatter buns?"

"Sure, Mama."

"Do you remember what we need?"

"I know they have raisins and something that makes them yellow," says Carl.

"Very good! A spice called saffron makes them yellow and it makes
the buns smell good, too."

"Lucia Day is tomorrow, girls, so get your jackets and boots off, and you can help us. You can bake the buns while I go out and pick the lingonberry leaves for Sofie's Lucia crown."

"Mama, I want to be Lucia too," Louise whines.

"You were Lucia last year. I know you'll make a perfect attendant this time, and Carl will be a wonderful Starboy."

"Mmm, this dough is yummy!" says Carl, licking his fingers.
"Don't eeeaaat it," shrieks Sofie.

"We need it for tomorrow," says Louise.

"Carl, you just take care of the raisins, Sofie and I will make the buns."

"Papa's home!"

"Hej, everybody! It sure smells like Christmas!"

"Can I try a Lussekatt bun?"

"Nej, Papa, They're for tomorrow!"

"OK, OK, I'll wait."

Mama says, "What are you laughing at? Is Papa making funny faces behind my back again? Remember, you children have to hurry and have supper now so you can get to bed early."

"Off you go. Papa and I will be in to say goodnight."

"We can't wait for tomorrow!" says Sofie.

"I'm going to sleep with my Starboy hat on," says Carl.

"You can't do that," Louise teases Carl, "your head will get pointed."

"Oh, I love Lucia Day. I remember how happy I was to be Lucia when I was young. But now we have a lot of work to do. Can you iron the gowns and Carl's shirt while I finish the Lucia crown?"
"Sure, I'd love to help."

12

"Wake up, Sofie, wake up, Louise, wake up, Carl!"
"Is it Lucia time already?" the children ask.
"Yes! It's December 13th, Lucia Day! Time to wake up Papa."

"Oh dear! What happened to all the pepparkakor, there are only two left!"

"We don't know," say Sofie and Louise.

"Do you know where the pepparkakor are, Carl?"

"Maybe Tomten or the cat or the dog ate them."

"Please tell me. I won't punish you, but we do need to find the cookies."

"I put some in my Starboy hat so they would be ready to give to papa and now they're all broken."

"Never mind, Carl, we can eat the crumbs. But next year, don't put them in your hat."

"Sofie, you first,
then Louise, and then Carl."

"Stop hitting me, Carl, or I'll tell Papa what you did with the pepparkakor," says Louise.

"Oh, you are such good singers, and the Lucia buns are wonderful
and I love the pepparkakor crumbs. Why don't you have some," says papa.
"Has Mama made some hot chocolate for you?
Shall we go to Grandma Gunhild and Grandpa Axel with
pepparkakor and Lussekatter?"
"Ja," the children yell.

"I'm going to teach Teddy the Lucia song." says Carl.

"Teddies can't talk." says Sofie.

"My teddy can sing."

Då i vårt mörka hus stiger med tända ljus Sancta Lucia, Sancta Lucia…

"Shhhhhh, we want to surprise Grandma and Grandpa."

"Are you ready?" Mama asks softly.

"OK, we're ready now," whispers Sofie. "Do you remember the words?" Sofie asks Louise and Carl.

"I'll copy you," Carl whispers back.

Papa rings the doorbell.
Grandma peeks through the peephole, unlocks the door and tiptoes back to bed.

"Sankta Lucia, Sankta Lucia…" The children sing. Grandpa is surprised and happy.
"Oh, you children must have practiced a lot!
You sound soooo good, and what wonderful bakers you are! Delicious!
Especially the crumbs."

"Children," asks Grandpa, "do you know why we celebrate Lucia Day?"

"No. Why, Grandpa?"

"When I was a child I was told that Lucia was a saint, a very good person who brought food to the hungry people in Sweden during the longest, darkest, winter night, a long time ago."

"That's right," says Grandma, "Sankta Lucia wore a crown with candles to brighten the dark days in Sweden. Now we bake the Lussekatter – Lucia buns – and give them to other people to remind us to be good like Lucia. Speaking of that, let's give some to our new neighbors. They just moved to Sweden from another country and they probably don't know about Lucia Day."

"Yes, let's give them some pepparkakor and Lussekatter!" Louise says.

24

"Thank you so much for doing this," says the neighbor.
"This is such a nice time and the children love it.
The buns and cookies are delicious."
"And I made the crumbs," says Carl proudly.

"It's almost time for school. You'd better get ready for the big Lucia performance for your teachers," says Mama.

"OK," they say, and kiss their grandparents goodbye.

"Tack så mycket," say Grandma and Grandpa.

"Next year, I'll be Lucia," says Louise to Sofie.

27

"Well," Mama says, "it looks like Lucia Day is over. You had such a big day and you were all wonderful! Put your gowns in the laundry room."

"Oh, we are so tired," says Sofie.

"Just have a little supper and go to bed."

The story of St. Lucia

The story of Lucia, the symbol of light amid the darkness for Sweden, has many different versions. Although her feast day is celebrated on December 13th in Sweden, she was born far away in southern Italy, in the third century A.D. It is said that she became a Christian after seeing her mother miraculously healed and she made a vow never to marry and to give the money that would have been her dowry to the poor. She refused to marry the man her family had chosen for her and some say he denounced her for her faith and was responsible for having her put to death. She died a martyr's death in 303 A.D. and was declared a saint. She is Santa Lucia to the Italians, Sankta Lucia to the Swedes, and St.Lucia, or St. Lucy, to all English speakers.

How the story of Lucia came to be such an important part of Swedish culture is somewhat of a mystery. Did the Vikings know of her and brought the legend to the North? Did monks and priests tell of her martyrdom? Of course, Sweden was once a Roman Catholic country and the stories of the saints were often told and retold in the Catholic religion. However, Sweden has been Lutheran for hundreds of years. It is not clear how the saint from Sicily became Sweden's beacon of light during the darkest period of the year, though one legend popular among Swedish Americans tells of a woman dressed in white standing in the bow of a boat crossing Lake Vänern. She was bringing food to the people of Värmland, who were dying of hunger during a famine many years ago. They say she wore a wreath in her hair, crowned with a ring of lighted candles. To this day, December 13th is one of the high points of the Christmas season and candles are lit all over Sweden to bear light against the darkness, as Lucia did.

Early in the morning of December 13th, the oldest daughter in the family in Sweden has the privilege of being the Lucia, wearing a long white gown sashed in red, with a wreath of lingonberry leaves on her hair. Candles – now usually run on batteries – are set into the wreath. Her sisters wear white gowns with tinsel in their hair and around their waists. Boys in the family wear tall pointed hats with stars on them. The "Starboys" traditionally are associated with the three wise men. The children awaken their parents and offer them coffee, saffron-flavored buns called *Lussekatter* and ginger snaps, called *pepparkakor*. Lucia programs are also held in schools, businesses and at public gatherings.

Lussekatter (Lucia buns)

1 pkg active dry yeast
1/4 c water, warm
3/4 c milk
1/2 c butter or margarine
1/2 c sugar
2 eggs
1/4 tsp salt
1/4 tsp powdered saffron
4 c flour

For brushing: 1 egg, 2T water
Dissolve yeast in warm water and set aside.
Warm milk, add butter to melt.
Place all above ingredients in a mixing bowl using 2 cups of the flour.
Mix for 3 minutes using mixer.
Add rest of flour and beat with wooden spoon.
Knead dough, adding a little flour for easy handling.
Put in a bowl and let rise to double.
Turn out on floured board and shape into Lussekatter.
Let rise on cookie sheet and brush with egg and water mixture before baking.
Put a raisin in each curl and bake at 450° for 10 minutes.
Makes about 4 dozen rolls.

Ginger snaps (Pepparkakor)

3 1/2 c flour
1 tsp baking soda
1/2 tsp salt
3/4 T ginger
2 tsp cloves
2 tsp cinnamon
1/2 c dark corn syrup
1 c butter
1c sugar
1 egg

Mix flour, soda and spices.
Heat syrup.
Melt butter and sugar in syrup.
Add egg.
Add dry ingredients to this mixture.
Put in cool place over night.
Roll out on board and cut into desired shapes.
Place on greased cookie sheet and bake at 375° for 10 minutes.

Both recipies are from Gunhild Anderson

45. Sancta Lucia.

Neapolitansk folkvisa

1. Nat - ten går tung - a fjät runt gård och stu - va.

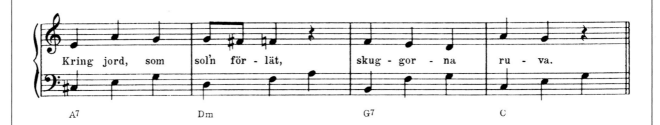

Kring jord, som soln för - lät, skug - gor - na ru - va.

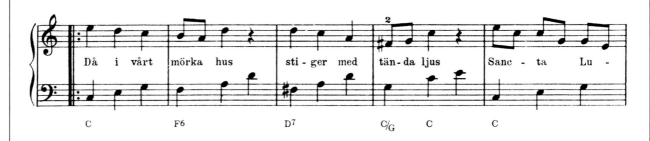

Då i vårt mörka hus sti - ger med tän - da ljus Sanc - ta Lu -

ci - a, Sanc - ta Lu - ci - a. Sanc - ta Lu - ci - a.

2. Natten är stor och stum.
   Nu hör det svingar
   i alla tysta rum
   sus som av vingar.
   Se, på vår tröskel står
   vitklädd, med ljus i hår
   Sancta Lucia, Sancta Lucia.

3. "Mörkret skall flykta snart
   ur jordens dalar."
   Så hon ett underbart
   ord til oss talar.
   Dagen skall åter ny
   stiga ur rosig sky.
   Sancta Lucia, Sancta Lucia.
   Arvid Rosén.

N. M. S. 1898

SANTA LUCIA

Lyrics: Arvid Rosén
Neapolitan folk tune
Translation: Anne-Charlotte Hanes Harvey
A singable translation

1. Night walks with heavy tread
round farm and byre,
dark sunforsaken earth
shadows attire.
Then in our winter gloom
candlelight fills the room:
Santa Lucia, Santa Lucia!

2. Silent and dark the night,
now hear descending

rustle of wings in flight,
all darkness ending.
Then she comes, dressed in white,
head wreathed in candles bright:
Santa Lucia, Santa Lucia!

3. "Shadows will soon be gone
from earth's dark valley" –
wonderful words anon
us cheer and rally.
Day will soon dawn anew
In skies of rosy hue:
Santa Lucia, Santa Lucia!

Easy Lucia or Starboy gown

Fold the piece of fabric or a sheet in half lengthwise. Fold it again crosswise. Cut the gown with center front and center back on the lengthwise fold, and the center of sleeve and shoulder on the other fold. Deepen the front neckline an additional 1" (2.5 cm).
Cut a 5" (13 cm) slit along the center front or the center back. Finish the slit and neckline with bias tape. At neckline, extend the bias tape at both edges to make ties. Stitch the side and sleeve seams. Hem the bottom and sleeve edges. Measurements given in diagram are in inches, 1" = 2.5 cm.

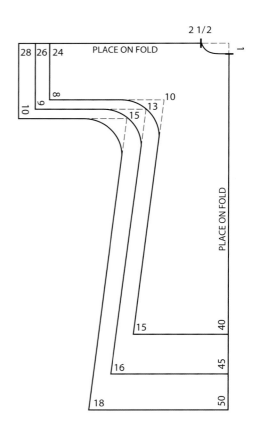

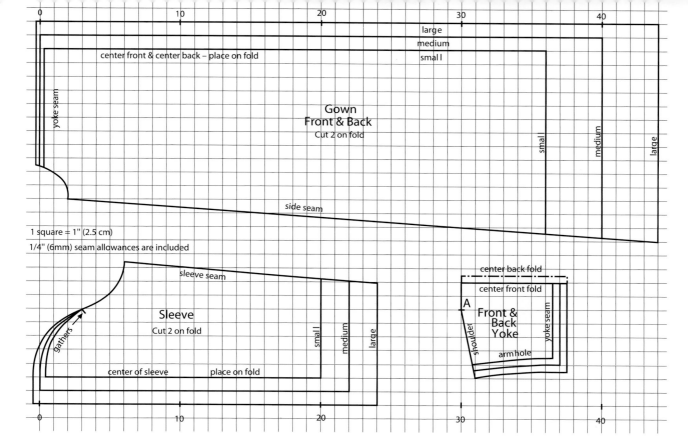

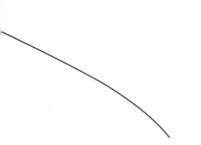

		Approx. Height of child	Length of gown at center back
Size	Small (4–6)	45" (115cm)	38.5 " (98cm)
Size	Medium (7–8)	50" (127cm)	43.5 " (110cm)
Size	Large (10–12)	56" (142cm)	48.5 " (123cm)
1 square = 1" (2.5cm)			
Neckline and collar are in full size. See page 36.			

Traditional Lucia gown

Make your pattern in full scale, following the diagram – easiest to use a tracing cloth with a grid.

On yoke, make one piece for the front and one for the back yoke. Match point A on the yoke to point A on the necklines and trace the front and back necklines. Trace the collar.

On the fold, cut two front yokes and two back yokes, (Yoke is double layers.) Cut two pieces for the gown (front and back), two sleeves, and four collars. Fold back yokes along back fold lines, wrong sides together, and press back edges. Stitch one front yoke to outside back yokes at shoulder seams. Stitch the other front yoke to the inside back yokes at shoulder seams.

Stitch two collars together at outside edge, turn right side out and press, repeat for other collar pieces. Pin collars to outside yoke at neckline with collar edges at center front and center back. Fold yokes at back edges, right sides together, with collar in between. Stitch neckline through all layers. Turn right side out. Fold yokes wrong sides together and overlap back edges 1" (2.5 cm) and stitch across to keep in place.

Gather yoke seams of front and back. Stitch yoke to front and back at yoke seams.

Hem sleeves with a narrow hem. Stitch a piece of elastic to sleeve 1" (2.5cm) above bottom edge, using a zigzag stitch. Gather cap of sleeves between marks. Stitch sleeves to armholes. Stitch front to back at side seams and sleeve seams.

Make buttonholes and sew on buttons to back yoke for closure, or use snaps.

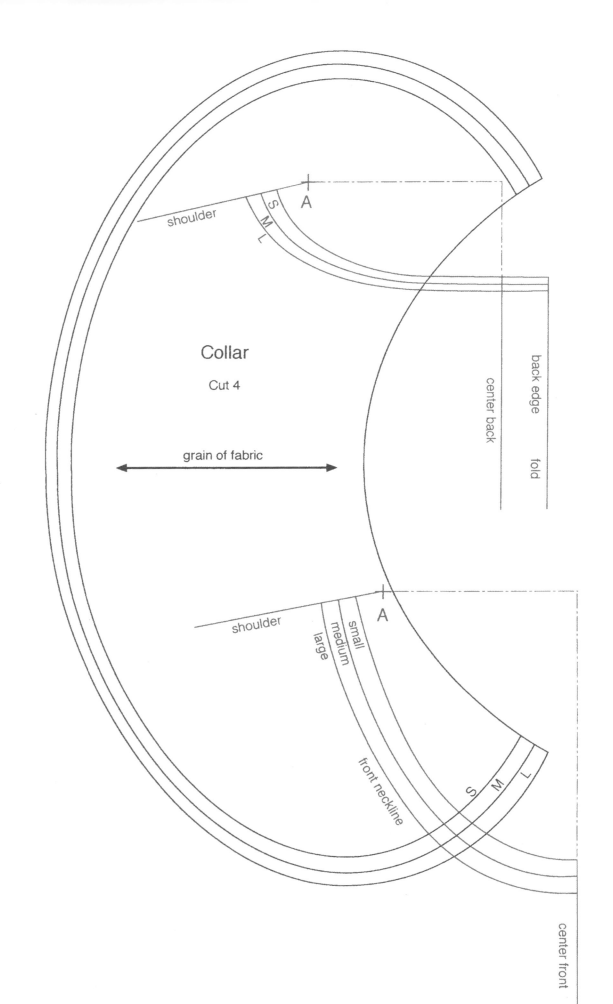

shoulder

S
M
L

A

Collar

Cut 4

grain of fabric

back edge

center back

fold

shoulder

small
medium
large

A

front neckline

S
M
L

center front